A Tale of
Two Donkeys

Malcolm Carter

Illustrated by Patty Naegeli

Published in the United States of America by
Half Halt Press, Inc.
P.O. Box 67
Boonsboro, MD 21713
www.halfhaltpress.com

Illustrations by Patty Naegeli

Printed in Mexico

Library of Congress Cataloging-in-Publication Data

Carter, Malcolm, 1935-
     A tale of two donkeys / Malcolm Carter ; illustrat-
ed by Patty Naegeli.
        p. cm.
     ISBN 0-939481-74-X
     I. Title.
     PS3603.A7777T35 2006
     813'.6--dc22

2006023775

This story of the two donkeys is a made-up one, but has been inspired by certain historical incidents in the New Testament. Who is to say it did not happen exactly as I have written it?

—Malcolm Carter

CHAPTER 1

The Fruitful Journey

The young donkey called Jenny was happy to plod slowly along the dusty road with Mary on her back and Mary's husband Joseph leading the way. Jenny was a beautiful soft gray color, with big brown eyes, long ears, and a kind, gentle expression.

The travelers had already walked 70 miles, from Nazareth to Jerusalem, and still had another three miles to go to reach Bethlehem, where they were headed.

The Roman Caesar Augustus had ordered an official count of all the people in Israel, called a census. Everyone had to register with his family in the town where he came from, and Joseph's family came from Bethlehem.

Their journey was especially slow because Mary was expecting a baby at any time and the bumpy ride on the donkey's back didn't help one bit. Mary and Joseph were kind to Jenny and she in turn tried to walk as steadily as she could to keep Mary as comfortable as possible. The final part of the journey was the hardest for the young donkey, because it was uphill all the way from Jericho. That's what the local people used to say:

Uphill to Jerusalem,
Downhill to Jericho.

It was a beautiful starry night and one star in particular shone with remarkable brilliance. As they reached Jerusalem, Mary began to feel strong sensations and she knew her baby would be born before too long. There were still a few miles before they reached Bethlehem and Joseph was feeling quite nervous. He knew it would be difficult to find a room for the night, especially at this late hour, but where was he going to find someone to help Mary deliver her baby?

Faithfully and surefootedly, Jenny plodded on, somehow understanding Joseph's worry (donkeys are very sensitive creatures), and in less than one hour, Bethlehem came into sight. Joseph tried the main inn of the town, but it was already overflowing with people who had come to register their families too.

The innkeeper was very apologetic when he saw how tired Mary was and how close she was to having her baby. As a last resort he said, "Look, sir, there's a shelter down the side of the inn; it's built into the rock. It's where we keep the animals our guests have ridden. I'm afraid it is a bit crowded but you can bed down there if you like. There is plenty of fresh straw and the well is just outside. I'm sorry I can't offer you more right now. We're run off our feet here in this place, but I'll ask my wife if she can spare a few minutes to look in on your good lady."

There was no time to lose because Mary's condition was becoming more serious, so Joseph gratefully led his wife and his donkey into the cave. A strong smell of animals met their noses as they entered. Joseph put Jenny into a stall with two other donkeys. Another stall held two camels and an ox. But at least it was warm from all the animals' breath.

Joseph quickly laid Mary down in some clean straw at the far end of the shelter. Gently he soothed her brow. The baby began to come quickly and Joseph realized that he was the midwife! There was no one else but him.

When the baby boy was born Joseph wrapped the newborn in the cloths Mary had packed and laid their child in fresh hay in the animals' feeding trough. The baby's cries subsided and he was soon asleep. Mary too was already asleep with exhaustion. Joseph stood and looked at them both, amazed at what had happened. The animals also knew something special had taken place that night.

When a baby's cry pierced the stillness of night,
It caused startled beasts to rear bolt upright.
The ox did yawn and to camels exclaim,
"What on earth was that, in heaven's name?"
The same query passed from jaw to jaw,
Till curious eyes, peering over, saw
The child in the hay, proud parents adore
Then Jenny, quite moved, intoned in awe:
"There's a stranger
In the manger!"

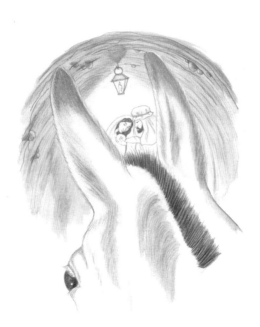

Over the next few days, Jenny watched from her stall her little family sharing the same shelter. Mary fed and sang sweet lullabies to her baby. She and Joseph had named him Jesus. Now Joseph was doing all he could to help in this poor accommodation. The innkeeper's wife came in several times with a meal and to help bathe the baby in a makeshift bath. She also promised to move them into a decent room in the inn when one became vacant.

Many other visitors had come, all so different, from half a dozen ragged shepherd boys to some wealthy Eastern travelers, whose camels were now in the next stall. It was all quite exciting. The animals in the stalls had a few questions too:

More camels arrived, ungainly but sure,
Bearing three kings whom star did allure.
Tired beasts are tethered within the byre,
While their owners, resplendent in royal attire,
Presented rare gifts upon their knees.
One camel in surprise did sneeze,
Another snorted while chewing cud:
"Why soil they thus their robes in mud?"
An answering whinny gave the ass,
"We are not sure what's come to pass,
But there's a stranger
In the manger!"

CHAPTER 2

On the Run

A few nights later, Jenny lay down with the other animals and had almost dozed off to sleep when she heard Joseph awaken Mary and say, "Mary, we must go quickly! An angel of the Lord has just come to me in a dream and warned that King Herod is going to search for our child to kill him!"

What? thought Jenny, Our baby? Who would want to hurt our beautiful baby boy? She was frightened and had already jumped to her feet when Joseph hurriedly opened her stall, saddled her up and led her out of the stable. Quickly Mary mounted her, cradling her baby, and Joseph led his fam-

ily out of Bethlehem. It was still dead of night and dark all around with no bright star in the sky this time.

The travelers journeyed for several days. Sometimes Jenny walked 15 miles in a day, occasionally 20. It was tiring for everyone, but Joseph was very gentle and made sure Jenny had plenty to eat and drink at each stopping place. At last they came to another country, called Egypt, where they knew they would be safe. They put up their tent and life became much easier. The baby boy was beautiful and had more settled nights. Jenny enjoyed her well-deserved rest too.

Then one day a traveler brought the news that the evil King Herod had died in Jerusalem. Now it was safe to begin the long return journey to their home in Nazareth.

CHAPTER 3

Falling on Hard Times

Mary and Joseph had now been away from their home for a few years. The baby Jesus was a toddler who loved playing with his pet donkey, Jenny. She loved the kind little boy, too, and sensed how special he was. As Jesus grew older, he would give rides on Jenny to other children in Nazareth. Jenny loved playing with those children too. Joseph became busy in his carpentry business and Jenny was just as happy carrying new ploughs, yokes, tables and chairs to customers. These were very happy years.

But sadly, about ten years later, fewer and fewer people ordered or bought Joseph's skilled handiwork. Everyone was poorer now because of the occupying Roman army. Joseph was worried. Where could he get more orders for his work? The only things he was selling were wooden beams to Roman soldiers, which they cruelly used to kill any Jews who opposed them. They did this by nailing them to the wood. It was a terrible sight.

By this time Jesus was twelve years old and had reached the age when every Jewish boy became a man in a special ceremony called *bar mitzvar*. Joseph and Mary didn't want their son to miss out on this very special day; it was very important. So Joseph borrowed some money and they set off as a family with their beloved donkey to journey once again to the capital Jerusalem for the *bar mitzvar* service. Two other families from Nazareth who had 12 year-old sons traveled with them.

They had a wonderful time. Jesus would never forget the moment he made his promises to God in front of his minister and quoted beautiful verses from the Bible. Thousands had come from all over Israel for the moving ceremony.

But Joseph knew that he had to sell their faithful donkey to make some money during this difficult time; he had no choice. He met a farmer at the animal market in Jerusalem and reluctantly sold Jenny to him for a good price.

Mary had tears in her eyes and Jenny, though she couldn't show her tears, was also upset to leave her little family. Jesus was broken-hearted and tearfully waved a sad goodbye to his four-footed friend.

CHAPTER 4

Life Down South

The farmer lived only a few miles away in Bethany and Jenny soon had another stall with lots of other donkeys. It was a wool farm. The farmer owned a large flock of sheep and, after shearing them, he packed the wool in large baskets, which were carried every week by the donkeys to market in Jerusalem.

Jenny was young and strong and soon made friends with the other animals plodding along with her. One male donkey in particular was very kind and handsome and over the next couple of years their friendship blossomed into love.

Some time later Jenny and her mate celebrated the birth of a baby foal. They called him Joel. What an unforgettable day that was! There was no choir of angels this time and no kings came to bring gifts to her stall, but like Mary, Jenny wondered what God had in store for her lovely son, Joel. Unknown to Jenny and her mate, Joel was going to play a remarkable part in God's plan.

The colt Joel grew up happily playing with his friends the sheep, becoming a handsome and strong young donkey, while his loving parents worked hard carrying the baskets of wool to market.

CHAPTER 5

Special Assignment

One day two strangers arrived at the sheep farm. Although Bethany was a long way from the sea or deep lakes, the men's clothes smelled of fish, which was unusual. What were these fishermen doing here? Jenny heard them talking to her owner, "Our master needs them both." Whatever the deal was, they all shook hands.

Before long both Jenny and Joel were saddled up and led by the two strangers for a few miles out of Bethany. They reached a group of a dozen young men with more fish smells coming from their clothes.

Their leader, smiling broadly, stepped forward to greet them and hugged Jenny, fondly stroking her muzzle. Jenny's heart began to pound! She knew this man! She recognized Jesus, now a full-grown man. Could it be that she and Joel had been sold back to him?

There was a large crowd too, of pilgrims and parents with their children, all heading towards Jerusalem for the big Passover Festival. Jenny sensed something special was going to happen, but she could never have imagined just how wonderful it would be.

Two of the fishermen threw their robes on Joel's back and Jesus mounted him and took the reins. As they started forward to take the road to Jerusalem, just a mile away, the crowd seemed to have grown even larger.

Joel was terrified as the people boxed him in and began to shout. On top of that, lots of them pulled palm leaves off nearby trees and began to wave them as they cheered Jesus.

Several placed palm leaves beneath Joel's feet. It was then that the singing started:

Hosanna, hosanna in the highest!
Blessed is he who comes in the name
of the Lord!
Peace in heaven and glory in the highest

The song was repeated over and over again. It was overwhelming, yet Joel's fear vanished as Jesus spoke quietly in Joel's ear and stroked the young donkey's neck with strong, gentle hands. Jesus was powerfully demonstrating that he didn't need any weapons or a warhorse. He was riding a baby donkey to make what it said in the Bible come true:

Look, your king comes to you riding on a donkey,
even on the foal of a donkey.

The walls of the great city came nearer and the singing went on and on. It was wonderful. It was unforgettable. Joel would remember this day for the rest of his life. So would Jenny, his proud mother who trotted slowly at the back of this amazing procession Jesus was showing everyone that He was the Prince of Peace.

And yet it didn't look very royal. Joel was so small and Jesus so tall that His feet almost scraped the ground! But Jesus was showing everyone that God's way was the way of peace. It was Jesus' greatest hour and Joel's too! Jesus dismounted at the city gates and lovingly stroked both Joel and Jenny before disappearing into the city, heading towards the temple. But the crowds carried on singing for a long time:

Hosanna, hosanna!
Blessed is he who comes in the name of the Lord!

CHAPTER 6

Separation

The sheer joy of that moment did not last. Joel was led back to the farm and was soon added to the pack animal team, carrying the baskets of wool to the market just like his parents. But his mother Jenny was taken directly to the Jerusalem market to be sold. She was getting too old to carry heavy bales of wool. Her working days were over. The sadness hit her because she had had no time to say goodbye to her lovely son or her mate.

Before long Jenny was sold in the market to a young doctor from Emmaus, a village outside Jerusalem. He had come with his wife, another Mary, to Jerusalem for the Passover Festival. Doctor Cleopas had promised his wife a gift for her birthday and Mary was thrilled with Jenny.

They were staying at a nearby inn in the heart of Jerusalem, so they took Jenny there and stabled her in the innkeeper's shelter, making sure she was comfortable. Jenny's face, as always, looked inscrutable, but inwardly she was desperately sad at the loss of her family. The next few days passed so slowly.

CHAPTER 7

Mission of Love

Then, on Friday morning, Jenny's long ears pricked up. Another crowd. More noise, but this time the words sounded harsh and angry. One word kept being shouted over and over: "Crucify!" Jenny heard the sound of a whip several times: someone was being lashed. Then the crowd moved on up the nearby hill.

Later, in the afternoon, another Joseph came to the inn and begged Jenny's new master, who was an old friend, to help him. It was urgent. Jenny was startled as both men burst into the stable and quickly saddled her. Jars of sweet-smelling ointment and rolls of cloth were stuffed into baskets slung over her back. They set off with Cleopas leading Jenny up the same hill as the crowd.

At the top of the hill were three large wooden crosses and on one of them a dead man was still nailed. Jenny began braying in alarm and sorrow as she recognized her life-long friend Jesus who had ridden on her son only a few days before. Now His body was battered and bleeding. Jenny reared to race away, but Cleopas and Joseph held her firm and tethered her to the foot of the Cross.

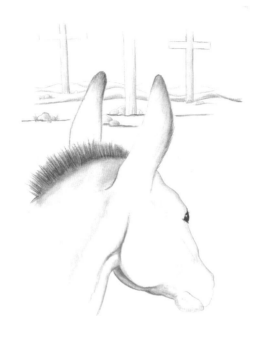

The men managed with great difficulty to lower Jesus' lifeless body onto Jenny's back. Slowly they led Jenny a short distance to the entrance of a cave where a few women friends and relatives of Jesus met them These included two more Marys, who caringly anointed Jesus' body with the precious ointments and wrapped Him in the cloths Jenny had carried. Then Joseph and Cleopas gently carried the dead Jesus into the tomb and with much help, including Jenny pulling on the rope, the gigantic stone at the entrance was rolled right across to seal the cave.

Everyone was tearful and sad, and they felt that their hearts were broken. No words were spoken.

The little crowd made their way back to the inn where Joseph and the two Marys left them. Jenny was stabled and given hay but she didn't feel like eating. The happiest day of her life had been quick-ly followed by her saddest.

CHAPTER 8

Journey into Life

Two days later, after the Passover Festival, Cleopas and Mary departed with Jenny to return to their village seven miles away. Deep sadness hung over all three of them, and for the first hour neither Cleopas nor Mary could think of anything to say. They passed large groups of armed Roman soldiers everywhere as they journeyed through the city. Once out into the country, they went over all that had taken place again and again Why had this terrible thing happened? Why?

They hardly noticed when a stranger emerged onto to their road and began walking alongside them. He asked them why they were so sad and downhearted. "Where have you been?" replied Cleopas. "Haven't you heard about the wonderful Teacher Jesus who was nailed to a cross two days ago?" His wife Mary said, "We are absolutely devastated, because we thought he was God's Chosen One who would save Israel and save us all."

The stranger didn't seem at all upset by what they said. Instead he gently reminded them of all the teachings in the Bible which clearly showed that the Promised Savior would suffer and be killed, but God would gloriously raise him to life again.

Cleopas and Mary were astonished by what the stranger said and before they knew it they had walked seven miles! Jenny was astonished, too! She pricked her long ears forward, because she recognized the voice of this stranger, even if she did not recognize His scarred face. It was her Jesus!

Their village Emmaus came into view. The stranger, as Cleopas and Mary still thought the man was, waved farewell and carried on walking, but Mary begged him to stay at their home and have a meal with them. "Come, sir, it's getting dark Please stay and eat with us." The stranger agreed and offered to stable the donkey while Mary and Cleopas quickly prepared a meal.

Jesus led Jenny into the stall adjoining the house and stroked her muzzle tenderly just as He had done a thousand times throughout her life. Jenny felt no tiredness, only joy and contentment. What memories of this man she had.

Jesus washed His hands and face and washed the dust from His feet before sitting down to the meal. Since He was a guest in their home, Jesus was invited to ask a blessing on their food. Reverently He picked up the loaf of bread, then broke it into two and said:

Blessed are You O Lord our God
Who brings forth food from the earth.

And that's as far as He got, because at that very moment, the stranger simply disappeared into thin air! Of course He was no longer a stranger to Mary and Cleopas: He was Jesus, their friend and Savior. They had clearly seen the nail marks in His hands when He picked up the bread to bless it. That was the moment they recognized Him. Now they knew He was truly risen from the dead. It was amazing! Cleopas and Mary hugged each other and Jenny in sheer joy.

No food was eaten that night. Instead Jenny was released from her stall and all three went trotting back to Jerusalem to tell their friends and, indeed, tell the world that Jesus was alive!

Jenny was thrilled to know her son had been part of this wonderful story. He had carried Jesus through the gates of Jerusalem. And she herself had been so vital at Jesus' birth and at His death

While Mary and Cleopas shouted excitedly to each other as they raced along, Jenny was also overjoyed, even if her inscrutable face didn't show it. She kept saying to herself, "My master needed my young son and my master needed me!"

It was a pity she couldn't see the cross now clearly marked on her back as reward for her pure and faithful love of Jesus. And indeed, to this day, the cross may be found on every donkey's back, as a sign of His love for all creatures, even a humble donkey.

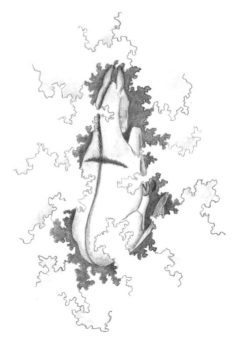